The Animals' Gift

The Animals' Gift

by Szabolcs de Vajay   illustrated by Lilian Obligado

SIMON & SCHUSTER BOOKS FOR YOUNG READERS
Published by Simon & Schuster
New York   London   Toronto   Sydney   Tokyo   Singapore

SIMON & SCHUSTER BOOKS FOR YOUNG READERS
1230 Avenue of the Americas, New York, New York 10020.
Text copyright © 1994 by Szabolcs de Vajay
Illustrations copyright © 1994 by Lilian Obligado
All rights reserved including the right of reproduction
in whole or in part in any form.
SIMON & SCHUSTER BOOKS FOR YOUNG READERS is a
trademark of Simon & Schuster.
The text of this book is set in 16 point Breughel.
The illustrations were done in watercolor.
Manufactured in the United States of America.
10 9 8 7 6 5 4 3 2 1
Library of Congress Cataloging-in-Publication Data
de Vajay, Szabolcs.   The animals' gift / by Szabolcs de Vajay ;
illustrated by Lilian Obligado.   p.   cm.
Summary: Ashba the donkey and his stablemate Ox try
to keep the baby Jesus warm after his birth in their stable.
[1. Jesus Christ—Nativity—Fiction.   2. Donkeys—Fiction.
3. Animals—Fiction.]   I. Obligado, Lilian, ill.   II. Title.
PZ7.D4958An   1994   [E]—dc20   90-46112   CIP   AC
ISBN: 0-671-72962-4

To our children,
Cristina and Sigismond

Ashba was a small gray donkey. He was a strong little animal, and he often carried heavy loads on his back. Ishmael was his master. Together, they lived on a small piece of land just outside the little town of Bethlehem. It was a quiet, peaceful place.

Ashba's home was a stable, which he shared with Ox. Both animals worked very hard, and at the end of the day, Ishmael filled the manger with crisp, sweet-smelling hay for them to eat.

Each day, Ashba and Ishmael awoke at dawn to start
working in the fields before the sun became too hot.

They worked together. Ishmael picked bunches
of grapes for making wine, and he loaded them
in large baskets for Ashba to carry on his back.

Ishmael also drew water from the well, and Ashba helped him by turning the great waterwheel. Around and around trotted Ashba, and around and around went the wheel. Up came fresh water.

At noon, they usually stopped to rest. Ishmael made a fire to cook himself a meal. Ashba nibbled contentedly on leaves and fruit from the bushes. They enjoyed this quiet companionship.

After lunch, they continued to work until sundown. As the sky grew dark and the town became still, Ashba and Ishmael slowly made their way back home. They were tired but content after a good day's work.

They had lived this way for many years, boy and
donkey. It was a simple existence in a small town.
Nothing extraordinary had ever happened.

But one cold winter evening as Ashba and Ishmael
were heading home, they saw a new star in the dark
sky, more brilliant than any they had ever seen. It
seemed to beckon to them.

As they reached the stable, Ashba and Ishmael saw
a man and woman waiting by the door.

"My name is Joseph, and this is Mary, my wife," the man explained. "Would you let us spend the night in your stable? There is no room for us at the inn."

They were shivering in the night air. Ishmael noticed that Mary was expecting a baby soon.

"Why are you traveling on such a cold night?" asked Ishmael. "And what brings you to Bethlehem?"

"Caesar Augustus has ordered everyone to return to his own city to be taxed. We live in Nazareth, but I belong to the House of David in Bethlehem. So we had to come here."

Ishmael smiled. "You are welcome to stay."

Mary and Joseph gratefully rested on the stable floor while Ishmael filled the manger with fresh hay for Ashba and Ox.

"I hope you will be comfortable. Good night." As Ishmael made his way back to his house in the dark, he glanced up at the night sky. The new star was shining directly over the stable.

Late that night, the baby was born. Joseph, Ashba, and Ox watched as Mary wrapped her newborn son in swaddling clothes and laid him in the manger on the soft, sweet hay. The animals were careful not to eat, for fear of disturbing the child.

Soon the little stable was a very busy place.

Shepherds from nearby fields arrived with their sheep. An angel, they said, had appeared before them in the sky, announcing the birth of the Savior in Bethlehem. A bright star in the east, he had said, would show them where they could find him. Ashba remembered the mysterious new star he had seen. The shepherds knelt before the manger and worshipped the child.

Ashba felt a cold wind blow on his back, and he turned to see three new visitors standing in the open doorway of the stable.

Three kings, dressed in richly colored robes, were seated on their camels laden with gifts of gold, incense, and myrrh. They, too, told of a star in the east that had guided them to the stable where the Savior had been born. They had journeyed from the far corners of the earth to find him. And now they, too, knelt before him in adoration and wonder.

Ashba turned to look at the child. He seemed to
be cold.

"Let's keep him warm," he whispered to Ox. So they stood low over the manger and breathed their warm breath on him.

And through the night, after all the visitors had left, and Mary and Joseph at last lay down to rest, the bright star shone over the stable and the animals kept watch over the child, keeping him warm.

The next morning, the sun rose as usual. As Mary, Joseph, and the child set out for the city, Mary gently patted Ashba and Ox. "Thank you," she whispered.

Another day began for Ashba and Ishmael. They went into the fields, where they would work until sundown, then slowly make their way home. It was a simple life in a quiet town. But something extraordinary had happened.